AM I LIKE YOU?

Designed by Patricia N Gonzalez

Printed in China

CPSIA Tracking Label Information:
Production Location: Guangdong, China
Production Date: 4/1/2016
Cohort: Batch 1

Library of Congress Cataloging-in-Publication Data available.
ISBN: 978-1-943645-03-9

10 9 8 7 6 5 4 3 2 1

TheCornellLab
Publishing Group

Produced by the
Cornell Lab Publishing Group
120A North Salem Street
Apex, NC 27502
www.CornellLabpg.com

MIX
Paper from
responsible sources
FSC® C124385
FSC
www.fsc.org

AM I LIKE YOU?

by **Laura Erickson & Brian Sockin**
pictures by **Anna Rettberg**

The**Cornell**Lab of Ornithology

I am myself.
That's a good thing to be.
There's nobody else
In the world quite like me.

The same goes for creatures
That live in the woods.
Each of them different,
Like us, as they should.

My mother and I
Love to wander around.
And visit with birds,
In trees and on ground.

Some birds are so friendly.
Some birds are so smart.
While others are bold,
Or make nests just like art.

We play a new game
Called "Am I like you?"
When we meet a new bird
And see what they do.

This game that we play,
Through the woods that we hike...
What birds are like us?
What birds are we like?

Ever hear of the early bird
That catches the worm?
It's the **robin** it's based on,
Of this we are firm.

I wake up real early,
And sing before dawn.
By first light I'm eating
All the worms on your lawn.

From autumn through spring,
I wander around.
Hanging out with my friends,
Wherever berries are found.

My kind don't mind blizzards,
And we cope with the heat.
We all stay together,
If there's plenty to eat.

Over there in a bush,
With a black and white suit,
We spy a young **chickadee**,
So small and so cute.

I'm curious and clever,
And I store food away.
Just in case I get hungry,
On a cold winter day.

I don't like to travel.
I stick to one place.
But if you are a stranger,
I'll show you my space.

Come join with my flockmates,
We'll hang out all day.
But I'm a loner come bedtime,
So at dusk, go away!

Up on a branch,
A red **cardinal** we see.
Don't get any closer,
Or he's likely to flee!

My song sounds like *"Pretty, pretty,*
Cheer cheer cheer cheer!"
It means, "This land is my land,
"You get out of here!"

If a scary big predator
Comes close to my nest,
I'll fly at it, and chase it.
I'm as brave as the best.

I suppose I seem cranky,
Living life my own way.
But if you are my family,
You can stay here all day.

Over there we see blue,
But we best keep our distance.
Jays are very protective,
Will defend in an instant.

Our feathers look great,
But our brains might be greater.
We stash away food,
And find it months later.

If you are a **Blue Jay**,
I will call you my friend.
But if you are an owl,
I will bug you no end.

I eat acorns and peanuts,
And suet that's sticky.
Also seeds, grains, and fruit,
I'm not very picky.

A **hawk** circles above,
Red tail on display.
Sharp eyes to the ground,
While he searches for prey.

I'm fiercely protective
Of my chicks till they're grown.
But the rest of the year,
I live all alone.

My vision is perfect,
From high in the sky.
I can spot a small rodent,
Even you, passing by.

If you are a mouse,
Then I have to be ruthless.
I kill with my talons,
Because I am toothless!

So small and so fast,
Like spies under cover.
Hummingbirds are so zippy,
But look still as they hover.

I'm so cute and so tiny,
Folks think I am sweet.
But I'm feisty and bossy,
I'm not what I eat.

I chase away animals,
Giant and small.
I don't like to share,
Not with any at all.

I spend my days flying,
From flower to flower.
And migrate long distance,
On sweet *flower power!*

Over there in the pond,
Two **geese**, there they are!
So silly they sound,
When they honk like a car.

I can get where I'm going,
On air, land, or water.
And we fly in the sky,
In a "V" shaped flight order.

A stray goose will get lonely,
But that won't last for long.
Other flocks will say "welcome,"
Come join in our song.

We're strong and bold too,
In big bunches we linger.
But don't get too close,
Or we'll nip at your finger!

Landing there in the lake,
Ducks waddle and quack.
Hey, here they all come,
They must want a snack!

I swim in the water,
Take walks in the park.
I nap when I want to,
By day or by dark.

I live in a flock.
We ducks stick together.
Eat, sleep, and be merry,
In good or bad weather.

I go bottoms up,
To catch food in a lake.
And I mooch food from people,
You give and I'll take!

Look over there!
Great Blue Heron we found.
Standing patiently quiet,
And not making a sound.

Do you ever go fishing?
Or try to catch frogs?
I can stand still for hours,
On the shore or on logs.

I am waiting for dinner
To come swimming on by.
Then I'll strike just like lightning!
And fishy, bye-bye!

My mate and I built
Our fine nest out of sticks.
Way up high in a tree,
Where we raise all our chicks.

We hear a sweet "coooo,"
From the barn roof above.
It could be a **pigeon,**
Or its cousin, the dove.

Some people don't like me,
They call me a rat.
Others keep me for racing,
I'm splendid at that.

I saved many soldiers,
A long time ago.
Now I must live near people,
'Cause that's all that I know.

I nest on your buildings,
On a farm or downtown.
If you toss out some breadcrumbs,
Then I'll quickly fly down.

It's getting towards dusk,
And an **owl** we hear.
Just a hoot, not a hollar,
And so wise they appear.

I spend the day roosting,
In a tree way up high.
I peek out to watch,
The world passing by.

At night I come out,
To catch moths and mice.
And I might take a bath,
To clean off some lice.

I have to be careful
If a big owl I see.
They have to eat too,
But I prefer it's not me!

It's time to go home,
And decisions are due.
But with so many birds,
Hard to pick one, it's true.

Each of them different,
In their own special way.
Just like everyone else,
Let me think, if I may.

What bird am I like?
What bird is like me?
A tough little Blue Jay?
Or a cute chickadee?

Maybe smart like an owl?
And I do love to talk.
Maybe brave like a cardinal?
And I see like a hawk.

My mom picked the robin,
'Cause she gets up real early.
She has so many friends,
And she never acts surly.

But today I feel silly,
Playful, fun and real loose.
Just don't get in my face.
Oh my gosh, I'm a goose!

What birds are you like?
What birds are like you?
Take the quiz and find out,
Cause that's what we do!

But never forget,
You're unique yes it's true,
And there's nobody else,
In the world quite like you.